February 2, 2005

Dear Jacob-
   Mommy and Daddy
can read this to
you. We all love
you!
          xxx
        Cousin
          Jane

To all the parents who love us,
and all the children who need our love.
Very special thanks to editor Michael Green,
whose vision made this book come to life. — M. K. C.

For Ann B. and Judith E. — S. I.

YOU ARE MY
I LOVE YOU

MARYANN K. CUSIMANO

illustrated by SATOMI ICHIKAWA

Philomel Books

I am your parent;
    you are my child.
I am your quiet place;
    you are my wild.

I am your calm face;
     you are my giggle.
I am your wait;
     you are my wiggle.

I am your carriage ride;
you are my king.

I am your push;
you are my swing.

I am your audience;
 you are my clown.
I am your London Bridge;
 you are my
  falling
   down.

I am your carrot sticks;
    you are my licorice.
I am your dandelion;
    you are my first wish.

I am your water wings;
   you are my deep.
I am your open arms;
   you are my running leap.

I am your way home;

  you are my new path.

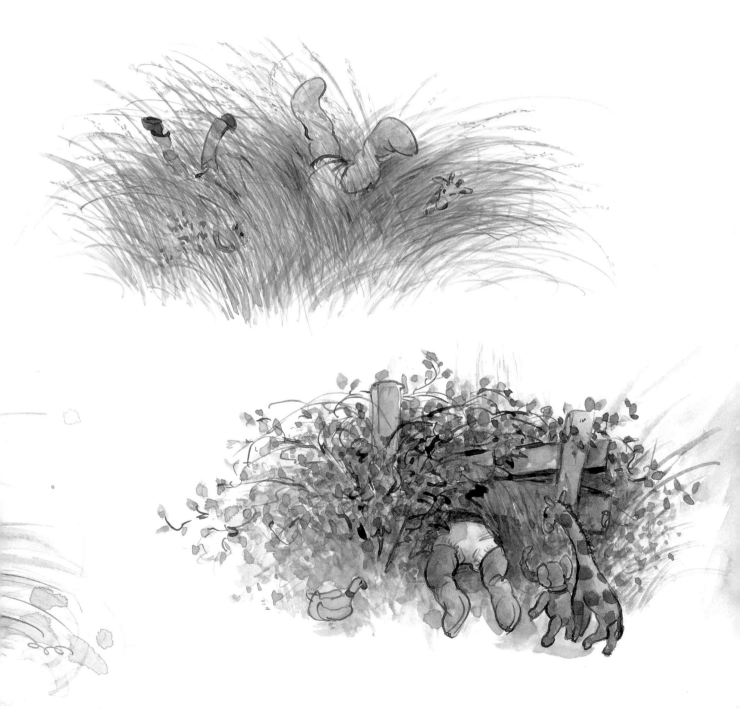

I am your dry towel;
you are my wet bath.

I am your dinner;
you are my chocolate cake.
I am your bedtime;
you are my wide awake.

I am your finish line;
     you are my race.
I am your praying hands;
     you are my saying grace.

I am your favorite book;
   you are my new lines.
I am your night-light;
   you are my starshine.

I am your lullaby;
you are my peekaboo.

I am your good-night kiss;
you are my
                    I love you.

Published simultaneously in Canada.
Manufactured in China by South China Printing Co. Ltd.
Book design by Gunta Alexander. Text set in Post Mediaeval.
The art for this book was painted in watercolor on Fabriano paper.

Library of Congress Cataloging-in-Publication Data
Cusimano, Maryann K. You are my I love you / by Maryann K. Cusimano ; illustrated by Satomi Ichikawa.
p. cm. Summary: Illustrations and rhyming text describe how a parent and child complement one another.
[1. Parent and child—Fiction. 2. Stories in rhyme.] I. Ichikawa, Satomi, ill.
II. Title. PZ8.3.C965 Yo 2001 [E]—dc21   00-057104   ISBN 0-399-23392-X
21 23 25 24 22 20